Who Gets to Ride

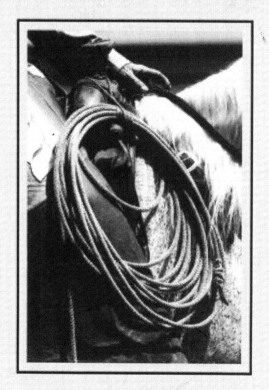

Cowboy Poetry

Robert R. Brown

BRAVE NEW GENRE, INC.

Publishers of Books, Music & Films

6535 N Palm Ave. #101

Fresno, CA 93704

www.bravenewgenre.com

Who Gets to Ride

© 2011 by Robert R. Brown

Library of Congress Control Number: 2010941254

Brown, Robert R.
Who Gets to Ride/Robert R. Brown
ISBN 978-0-9820474-4-6

1. Cowboy Poetry   2.Western Poetry
3. Old West—Fiction   4. American West—Fiction
5. Gunfighting -- Fiction 6. American Cowboy – Fiction

Edited by Bonnie Hearn Hill.

Cover by Larry Hill.

Print-on-demand and E-book editions of this book are available through *www.bravenewgenre.com*.

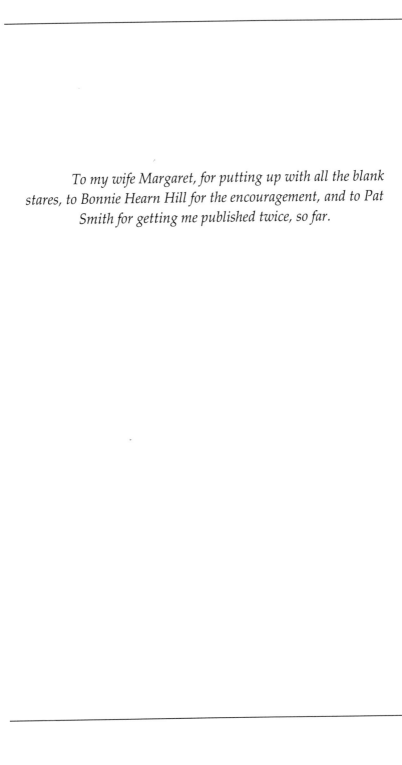

To my wife Margaret, for putting up with all the blank stares, to Bonnie Hearn Hill for the encouragement, and to Pat Smith for getting me published twice, so far.

Table of Contents

I.

Sometimes a man must crawl.

Sometimes a man must stand.

II.

and the memory will haunt you

through the years as you grow old.

Table of Contents

III.

But I think we'll travel on a bit,

beyond those mountains there.

And maybe find a better place.

There must be one somewhere.

IV.

Who would have thought that an innocent kiss,

would lead to my world going crazy like this?

V.

Charlie used to ride them bulls,
but me, I had more sense.
While he was out there riding,
I was sitting on the fence.

I.

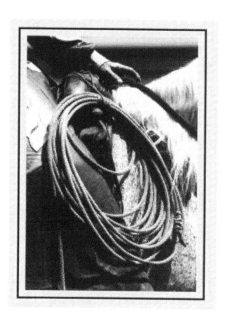

Sometimes a man must crawl.

Sometimes a man must stand.

OLD PETE SMITH

Old Pete Smith was a quiet guy
   who swept out the Union Bank.
He stayed away from trouble
   and seldom ever drank.

The town folks all ignored him
   when he shuffled down the street,
but he always took his hat off,
   if a lady he did meet.

Then one day the Doolin Gang
   came riding into town.
They started drinking whiskey
   and went swaggering around.

The marshal was a has-been,
   whose hero days were through.
He laid his badge upon his desk
   and quietly withdrew.

And as the marshal rode away,
           the gang laughed loud and long.
The town folks all were worried,
           fearing what else might go wrong.

Then Doolin saw the Union Bank
           and said, "We need some dough."
So when the gang was gathered up,
           he said, "Come on. Let's go."

Now Old Pete Smith was sweeping,
           when the Doolin Gang walked in.
He swept some dirt on Doolin's boots,
           and trouble did begin.

For Doolin had a vicious streak.
           He liked to cause a scene.
Whenever someone made him mad,
           Bill Doolin got plumb mean.

He snarled and swore at Old Pete Smith,
           then knocked him to the floor.
He said, "Old man, wipe off my boots,
           then crawl out through that door."

For a moment, Pete just lay there,
> then, without a word to say,
he pulled out his bandanna
> and wiped that dust away.

Then slowly on his hands and knees,
> out through the door he crawled,
while Doolin laughed his crazy laugh,
> then in a loud voice called,

"Don't no one move. You won't get hurt.
> Just give us all the money.
Then lay face-down upon the floor
> and don't try nothing funny."

They took the money, every cent,
> then quickly backed outside,
where Doolin said, "Mount up, boys.
> I think it's time to ride."

But in the street stood old Pete Smith,
> a pistol in each hand.
He said, "Sometimes a man must crawl.
> Sometimes a man must stand."

Those pistols started in to speak
      a message clear to all.
And there around Bill Doolin,
      his men began to fall.

The bag of gold in Doolin's hand
      dropped quickly to the ground.
And before he got his pistol out,
      his men were all shot down.

He saw that old man watching him
      with washed-out pale blue eyes.
He said, "When someone crosses me,
      that someone quickly dies."

Then lightning fast, he drew and fired,
      but the bullet just went wide.
For when he shot at Old Pete Smith
      was when Bill Doolin died.

The town folk now take notice
      when Pete wanders down the street.
They all smile and say to him,
      "Good morning, Marshal Pete."

THE MEMORIES THAT HAUNT ME

I killed a man two years ago,
    and ride to find some place I can forget.
But summers come and winters too,
    and the place I'd hoped to find, I haven't yet.

The lonely trails grow lonelier,
    and the wind blows ever colder on my back.
The mountains all grow steeper,
    as I ride along each narrow, unused track.

The memories that haunt me
    seem to have no trouble finding where I've gone
And each evening by my campfire,
    they whisper that it's time that I move on.

Though sometimes I don't listen,
    for my pony needs to eat and then to rest.
But those memories grow stronger
    'til I just can't stand the aching in my chest.

As I'm sitting here this evening,

> wishing time would somehow heal my broken
> heart,

I realize that healing,

> isn't something that my running can let start

So I know that I must go back,

> where the loneliness within me all began.

And there I'll have to find her,

> and ask her to forgive me if she can.

For it was a pretty woman,

> who somehow made a lifelong friendship end

on the dusty streets of Dallas

> when I drew my gun and shot down my best
> friend.

DADDY'S PISTOLS

When my momma met my daddy,
          he was known both far and wide,
as a fast man with his pistols,
          and a couple of men had died.

He was just a small-town marshal,
          but most outlaws rode on by,
for they knew that if they faced him,
          chances were that they would die.

Her blue eyes made him happy
          in a way he'd never known.
He told her that he loved her,
          and soon took her for his own.

He quit the marshal's office
          six short months before I came,
when she told him that my daddy
          couldn't wear a gunman's name.

He put away his pistols,
        and then studied for the law.
But the day he hung his shingle,
        was the last day that he saw.

Some outlaws still remembered
        how he'd made them run away.
And he didn't have his guns on
        when one came to town that day.

He was standing on a ladder
        when that coward gunned him down,
then jumped upon a waiting horse
        and thundered out of town.

I remember ten years later,
        Mama still went every day,
to stand there by his headstone
        just before she knelt to pray.

And she'd ask him to forgive her
        for she felt she'd done him wrong,
when she made him hang his guns up
        when she should have made him strong.

When I wasn't quite yet fourteen,
  I would practice my fast draw,
after sneaking Daddy's pistols out,
  while making sure Ma never saw.

Then the day I that turned sixteen,
  I ran away from home.
And I took those pistols with me
  as I started out to roam.

I was looking for the killer,
  who had gunned my daddy down.
And I practiced with those pistols,
  as I moved from town to town.

Well, I found him in El Paso,
  in a Mexican café,
And I stood there and I watched him
  as he put the booze away.

Of course he didn't know me,
  but I still could see him shake.
I knew that if I killed him,
  it would be a bad mistake.

For I looked into the mirror,
      where I met his bloodshot gaze.
I could see he lived in terror,
      and would for all his days.

I took off Daddy's pistols,
      then hid them in my pack,
and I found my momma waiting,
      on the street when I got back.

When she asked me if I'd killed him,
      I was speechless for awhile.
When at last I said I hadn't,
      then I finally saw her smile.

A lot of folks were watching,
      when she held me close that day.
"Welcome home," she whispered,
      "Now, go put those guns away."

THE BARLOW RAID

Pa and Charlie White were talking
      out behind the shed,
and though they kept their voices low,
      I heard what Charlie said.

He said, "They raided Barlow's place,
      and Henry's sure to die.
We wouldn't even know it yet,
      if I hadn't happened by.

"His wife is gone, his horses too.
      Their signs all headed west.
We need someone to follow signs,
      and God knows you're the best.

"I don't think they'll come up this way,
      cause they know who you are.
They won't want to face you,
      though you've taken off the star."

At first Pa said he couldn't go.

        He had to stay with me.

But Charlie said, "Ben Stone is one.

        He's somehow gotten free."

I saw Pa's face go sickly white.

        His eyes turned fierce and mean.

He didn't look like Pa at all.

        A look I'd never seen.

He didn't say much after that,

        just saddled up his horse,

and when I asked if I could go,

        he told me no, of course.

He said, "You go to Charlie's house,

        and stay with Mrs. White.

It's likely we'll be gone awhile,

        and won't get back tonight."

But I was mad because he said

        I couldn't go along,

so I decided I'd stay home,

        while knowing it was wrong.

I had a fort built in the trees,
      where I played every day,
and I thought that I'd just stay out there,
      while Pa was gone away.

But just in case, I moved a chair,
      and got Pa's shotgun down,
though I wasn't supposed to touch it
      when he was not around.

I played at fighting renegades,
      and killed a dozen men,
though some of them I'd killed before
      and had to kill again.

While I pretended I must hide
      from outlaws sneaking round,
somewhere in that grove of trees,
      I heard a funny sound.

Then two strange men came sneaking up
      to peer out at the house,
while I made sure my breathing
was as quiet as a mouse.

One said, "I don't believe he's here.
    That horse of his is gone.
Maybe we should give this up
    and just keep moving on."

The other said, "He locked me up,
    and sent me to the pen.
I knew that he'd be on my trail,
    if I messed up again.

"When I got out, I ambushed him,
    but missed and killed his wife.
I turned and ran away that day
    to try to save my life.

"and I was in the Juarez jail,
    before he tracked me down.
I heard they told him I would hang,
    and that's why he left town.

"When he finds out I'm on the loose,
    he'll never let me be.
This time I'm going to do it right.
    It's either him or me.

"We'll just fort up inside the house,
      and wait 'til he walks in.
When he's dead, then I'll be sure,
      he won't bother me again."

I thought that they might hear my heart,
      cause it was beating hard.
But I stayed still and shivered,
while they sneaked across the yard.

I knew they planned on killing Pa,
      and wondered what to do,
as they went into our cabin
      and disappeared from view.

I had to somehow go find Pa,
      and tell him they were there,
but couldn't figure out a way
      to find out when or where.

Cause I remembered Charlie's words
      about tracking someone down.
And that meant they'd be out on the trail,
      not headed into town.

But if these were the men, who raided
  Barlow's place today,
then the horses that they'd stolen,
  couldn't be too far away.

I dragged along Pa's shotgun,
  as I crawled on hands and knees,
'til I was sure they couldn't see me
  through the brush and trees.

At last I found the horses,
  and found Mrs. Barlow too.
They'd tied her to a Pinion tree
  that kept her hid from view.

Her eyes went wide in shocked surprise
  to see me standing near.
And I could tell that she was nearly
overcome with fear.

The rope was stiff and hard to move,
  but somehow it came free,
and I was glad that no one saw
  while she kept hugging me.

I handed her Pa's shotgun,
        as I told her what I'd heard.
She made me tell it all again,
        repeating every word.

She said, "They think my Hank is dead,
        and no one knows, but me.
And given time, they'd have killed me too,
        except you've set me free.

"They didn't try to hide their tracks,
        so your Pa will come this way.
You take a horse and look for him,
        while I make sure they stay."

She helped me on a big black horse,
        and pointed where to go,
and I rode hard the way she said,
        for half an hour or so,

'til I met Pa and Charlie White,
        and several other men,
and told them what had happened,
        as we headed back again.

I told them Mrs. Barlow
        wouldn't let those outlaws run,
but I didn't bother saying
        that I'd given her Pa's gun.

Pa made me stay with Charlie White,
        while he went on ahead.
It wasn't long 'til he came back,
        and this is what he said.

"I don't know how it happened,
        cause she's crying hard right now,
but she must have gone up to the house
        and got inside somehow.

"She grabbed down that old shotgun,
        that I keep above the door,
then shot them both in self defense,
        and they won't kill no more."

FRONTIER DAUGHTER

Pa had still been conscious
　　　　when he told her what to do,
warning her he might pass out
　　　　before the job was through.

He'd carefully explained each step,
　　　　like how to heat the knife.
And said she'd have to do it,
　　　　if she hoped to save his life.

She'd somehow done just what he'd said,
　　　　and cut the bullet free,
then cauterized the wound, that through
　　　　her tears, was hard to see.

She stayed right by his side,
　　　　until at last he seemed at ease,
then did those things she had to do,
　　　　despite her trembling knees.

She put their bloody clothes to soak,
        then loaded every gun.
She didn't stop to rest until
        all her chores were done.

Next morning she washed out the blood
        from her dress and daddy's shirt,
and those cloths she'd used for bandages,
        where blood had mixed with dirt.

She was hanging them upon the line,
        and reaching for her gown,
when a movement in the distance,
        caught her eye and brought a frown.

Though heat waves made things waver
        so she couldn't see him well,
a man was walking toward her
        through the sage and chaparral.

He was coming up the same trail
        that the other two had used,
though the fact that he was walking
        made her feel confused.

There was nothing there but desert,
    for at least two hard days ride,
and the man that she was watching
    had a long and steady stride.

She paused for just a moment
    as she watched him drawing near,
and the fact he had a rifle
    only added to her fear.

So she hurried to the cabin
    where her Pa still lay in bed,
weakened from the bullet wound
    that nearly left him dead.

She stretched to reach the shotgun
    on its rack above the door,
and shuddered when she touched it
    like she'd never done before.

She peeked out through the gun port
    that was built into the wall,
and as she watched the man approaching,
    she could tell that he was tall.

She felt her fingers tremble
        as she eased the hammer back,
then hid the gun behind her
        as she stepped out from the shack.

But he didn't look much older
        than her nearly seventeen,
though his shoulders were much broader
        and his body hard and lean.

His face was smeared with sweat-streaked dirt,
        but his eyes were clear pale blue
and as he looked at her, she wondered,
        what a man like him would do.

"May I help myself to water?"
        he politely asked her first,
then he headed for the horse-trough,
        where he meant to slake his thirst.

But when he saw the horses
        that were standing in the pen,
he abruptly stopped and turned around,
        and stared at her again.

This time his face looked harder,
      as she heard him softly say,
"That black horse standing yonder,
      who rode him yesterday?"

She swallowed hard and tried to speak,
      but her throat was much too dry.
Yet she knew she had to answer,
      so she made another try.

"Are they friends of yours?" she asked him,
      while she gripped the shotgun hard.
"Not hardly," was the answer,
      as he looked around the yard.

"Three men tried to rob me
      just past sun up yesterday.
It was more by luck than anything
      that I somehow got away.

"Their first shot hit my horse real bad,
      but he didn't let me down.
He carried me to shelter
      before he crumpled to the ground.

"They were close behind me,
          and one won't kill no more.
Now I'm looking for the other two,
          to even up the score."

She hoped that she could trust him,
          as she told him, " They're both dead.
I haven't had time to deal with them.
          They're out there in the shed.

"Pa made me go inside the house,
          when they first came into sight.
He didn't want them seeing me,
          'til he knew that'd be all right.

"They just helped themselves to water,
          then sprawled out in the shade,
and told Pa they needed horses,
          but he said he wouldn't trade.

"I saw the whole thing happen
          through the gun-port, from inside,
as the tall one drew his pistol
          and shot Pa in the side.

"I grabbed down Pa's old shotgun
　　　as soon as I saw him drop.
I'm sure they would have killed him,
　　　if I hadn't made them stop."

"Pa had me dig the bullet out,
　　　but I can't do no more.
I sure could use your help, because,
　　　I never killed no one before."

EMMA

I'd killed a gambler called Jack Reed,
      who used a crooked deck,
so they had me on the gallows,
      with a noose around my neck.

The fight had been a fair one;
      there was little doubt of that,
for he drew first and shot at me,
      but only hit my hat.

But I was just a stranger,
      on my way to passing through,
while he had many friends a-telling
      others what to do.

The man who seemed to be in charge,
      said, "Let's be sure we're right.
Does anybody know why we
      can't hang this guy tonight?"

"I've got a couple reasons,"
> said a soft voice from the crowd.
And it seemed to carry clearly,
> though it wasn't very loud.

A couple cowboys stepped aside,
> to let a woman by,
for the sawed-off shotgun that she had
> looked deadly to the eye.

"Now Emma, why are you here?"
> asked the man who'd tied the noose.
"I'm here to see you do what's right,
> and turn this stranger loose."

She said, "It doesn't matter,
> if you liked Jack Reed or not.
You know darn well he cheated,
> and deserved just what he got.

"Now, my finger's getting nervous,
> so don't make me wait too long.
You'd better cut this stranger free,
> or something might go wrong.

"His horse is tied out back," she said,
       "and I've one more thing to say.
I'll be riding with him,
       to make sure he gets away."

We thought we might be followed,
       so we rode hard for a while,
but the lack of dust behind us,
       let me face her with a smile.

"I don't know why you did it,
       but I sure owe you a lot.
Though I've very little money,
       you can have all that I've got."

She said, "Right now we're even,
       though there's something you can do.
If you'll take me home to Houston,
       I'll end up owing you."

She sat there for a moment,
       as she stared at her left hand,
then pulled a gold ring from her finger,
       and dropped it in the sand.

She said, "I was a young girl,
      when Jack Reed rode into town,
and made me feel important,
      by escorting me around.

"So I married him last August,
      and stopped loving him right then.
Now, thanks to you he'll never ever
      beat me up again."

STALLION

I turned fourteen that very week
         and felt I was full grown,
cause Pa's birthday present for me
         was a rifle of my own.

We were ranching in Wyoming
         where we had a little place,
when some mares that we were growing
         disappeared without a trace.

Pa's horse had slipped and fallen
         and Pa's leg was broken bad,
so for me to try to find them
         was the only chance we had.

Pa said, "I couldn't sleep last night.
         My leg done throbbed a bit.
I thought I heard a stallion scream
         before that rainstorm hit.

"I ran across some Mustang tracks,

  a week or so ago,

at that spring up north of Rodger's ridge

  where those Lodge pole saplings grow.

"You take your rifle with you,

  and go ride up that-a-way.

Make sure you take enough supplies

  for at least a full week's stay.

"Our mares have all got shoes on.

  They'll be easy enough to spot.

And I don't have to tell you,

  they're the best stuff that we've got.

"We can't afford to lose them,

  so go see what you can find.

And if that stallion's got them,

  then build yourself a blind.

"It may be several days before

  he leads them in to drink,

But the sign said they come often,

  or at least that's what I think.

"Now, I don't like shooting horses,
        but he'll steal every mare we've got,
so I won't feel free and easy,
        until that stallion has been shot."

Well, I knew that if I didn't go,
        Pa would go instead,
when what he really needed
        was to stay at home in bed.

I found those tracks just like he said,
        some made since last night's rain.
And scattered there among them,
        were shod tracks showing plain.

So I built myself a real good blind
        and settled down to wait.
I figured they would come at dawn,
        or in the evening late.

I lay there chewing jerky
        for what seemed like half the night.
Then the sound of hoof beats woke me up
        as the morning sky grew light.

I saw that stallion prancing
      as he brought the whole herd in.
I recognized some mares of ours
      and counted at least ten.

His mane was blowing in the wind,
      his tail streamed out behind.
A prettier sight than what I saw
      would sure be hard to find.

And I felt my heart near breaking
      as I focused through my sights,
but Pa had put his trust in me
      to do this one job right

As I slowly squeezed the trigger
      and my adult life began,
I found I didn't like the fact
      that I was now a man.

II.

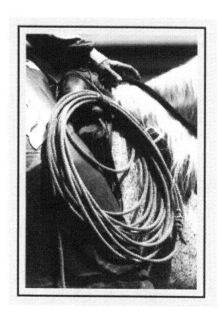

and the memory will haunt you
through the years as you grow old.

MYSTERIOUS MAIDEN

In the Superstition Mountains,
      where the Dutchman's mine is lost,
and the twisted trails and canyons
      make the gold not worth the cost,

There's a maiden dressed in buckskin,
      who is seen by very few,
but she leaves a burning question
      in the minds of those who do.

For she leads a painted pony,
      with an old man on its back,
whose sightless eyes keep staring
      at a world that's always black.

The rattlesnakes don't rattle
      as the two go drifting by,
though the buzzards all come wheeling
      to that lonesome stretch of sky.

If you ever ride those mountains,
      then perhaps one day you'll meet,
that pretty dark-haired maiden,
      with the buckskin on her feet.

But she'll leave no tracks behind her,
      as she rounds the nearest bend,
and the only sound you'll hear,
      is the sighing of the wind.

And if you round the bend behind her,
      you will stop and stare in awe,
as the empty trail before you,
      makes you wonder what you saw.

Other cowboys that you meet there,
      say they never saw the pair,
of the blind man and the maiden
      with the long black braided hair,

Your searching eyes will tell you
      what your mind already knows,
That they're nowhere on that trail,
      and there's no place they could go.

Though the sun is shining brightly,
        you will shiver from the cold,
and the memory will haunt you
        through the years as you grow old.

GRANDPA JED

I fought with Billy Simpson,
      cause he killed my Grandpa Jed.
When our bloody fight was over,
      it left Billy Simpson dead.

Then his brothers got me cornered
      in a building there in town.
They said I'd have to face them,
      or they'd burn that old shack down.

So I told them I would meet them
      upon the main street after dawn.
With the odds at three to one,
      I figured any chance was gone.

I sat there in the darkness
      with my back against the wall,
determined I would do my best,
      before they saw me fall.

I remembered Grandpa Jed,
      and all the things he'd taught to me.
Then I thought I heard his voice say,
      "I could let you have all three.

"But since it's my fight you are fighting,
      I'll be standing there with you.
Be sure you take the right-hand one.
      I'll take the other two."

I felt my head fall forward,
      so I shook myself awake.
To dwell upon the dream I'd had
      would be a big mistake.

As the sky began to brighten,
      telling me that dawn was near,
I tried to make myself stay calm
      and overcome my fear.

I double-checked my pistol,
      then stepped out on the street,
and walked toward the town center
      where all four of us would meet.

But when I saw them coming,
      I remembered Grandpa's voice,
and though I felt a little foolish,
      the right one was my choice.

Then the guns began to thunder,
      and the air filled up with smoke.
I had no time to think about
      the words that Grandpa spoke.

In a moment, it was over,
      and the three lay on the ground.
I stood there as the town folks
      all came out to gather round.

But all that I could think about
      was Grandpa Jed's advice,
and the fact all three of them were down,
      when I had only fired twice.

SWEET KATHLEEN

The cowboys gathered round the fire
          every Halloween,
and told their scary tales of ghosts
          and other things they'd seen.

But Hugo Binder wouldn't come,
          no matter what was said.
If someone asked if he was scared,
          he'd slowly shake his head.

Then one gloomy Halloween,
          he said, "Tonight I've come,
just to tell my story,
          though it's not as bad as some.

"I used to date a pretty girl.
          I called her Sweet Kathleen.
I took her for a buggy ride,
          one cloudy Halloween.

"I drove down by the graveyard,
          just so she would hold me tight.
A willing girl, a blanket,
          everything was going right.

"Then ghostly looking figures
          floated up from every grave,
but I refused to drive away,
          just to prove that I was brave.

"Kathleen began to shiver,
          as I tried to hold her near,
and her ruby lips were trembling
          as she whispered in my ear.

'That looks like Uncle Rudolph.
          He passed on years ago.
And that must be Aunt Matilda,
          though her face is white as snow.

'And there's my cousin Jacob.
          He was killed at Bunker Hill.
And my baby brother Henry.
          Mama cries about him still.'

"Well, I'd seen enough of shadows,
       so I turned that rig about.
But she said, 'No. Wait a second.
       The moon is coming out.'

"Well, sure enough, that moment,
       the clouds began to thin.
And a full moon soon was shining,
       as she hugged me close again.

"I could feel her curves against me,
       and her fingers in my hair.
So I pulled back hard upon the reins
       to keep that buggy there.

"Her soft breath blowing in my ear,
       made me a trembling wreck.
So I couldn't move a muscle,
       as her fangs sunk in my neck."

When Hugo finished talking,
       not a cowboy made a sound.
So he stood and took some steps away,
       then slowly turned around.

He said, "That's why on Halloween,

    I never hang about.

And I guess I'd better go now,

    cause the moon is coming out."

ANCIENT MEMORIES

I'd ridden hard for several days.
       My horse was tuckered out.
So I hunted for a camping place
       with lots of grass about.

I found one in a canyon,
       where some ancient ruins stood
near a spring-fed pool of water
       and a fair supply of wood.

A storm was blowing on the wind.
       I thought that it might snow.
And though the place was spooky,
       there was no place else to go.

That ruin offered shelter,
       so I picked an empty room
where my small fire lit the corners
       and chased away the gloom.

Late that night while sleeping,
       I heard the tom-toms beat.
And the rhythm of those beating drums
       soon brought me to my feet.

The room where I was standing
       wasn't empty any more.
There were baskets, jugs and scattered bags
       and beds upon the floor.

And through the open doorway,
       I could see the dancers sway,
and the magic of the moment
       quickly led me out that way.

Where I joined with the dancers,
       making steps I didn't know,
Though that didn't seem to matter
       as I let my body go.

I danced what seemed like hours
       'til exhaustion claimed my mind,
and I stumbled to my bed-roll
       which was there for me to find.

Early the next morning,
       in the sober light of day,
that room was once more empty.
       Everything had gone away.

When I thought of maybe moving on,
       my horse soon changed my mind.
A better place for him to rest
       would sure be hard to find.

That night I once again woke up
       and walked that canyon floor
And mingled with the people there
       just like the night before.

I found that I had memories
       of a place I'd never been
and walked on ancient pathways
       I would never walk again.

I held a woman to me
       who I loved with all my heart,
and knew that she would miss me
       when we had to be apart.

At daylight I caught up my horse
       and loaded up my gear,
while listening for ancient drums
       I knew I wouldn't hear.

I quickly rode away from there
       and never turned to look,
and knew I wouldn't recognize
       the trails that I took.

And when I gaze into a campfire now,
       it sometimes makes me sad,
for I know that I have memories
       of dreams I never had.

ANCIENT RUIN

I was riding by a canyon
        I had not been in before,
when I felt a sudden urge
        to take time to go explore.

The stream that wandered through it
        let the trees grow straight and tall,
where I saw an ancient ruin
        high upon the canyon wall.

I had never heard it mentioned
        in the stories that were told,
But I knew beyond a doubt
        the place was very old.

I felt I couldn't ride away
        before I looked inside,
and saw that place where men had once
        been born and lived and died.

I had to rope a jutting rock
          to climb up to a ledge,
then felt my heartbeat quicken,
          as I teetered on the edge.

And when I reached the buildings
          that were in a shallow cave,
I knew whoever lived there,
          had been both strong and brave.

I peeked in through a doorway,
          but the place was filled with gloom,
so I made a torch and used it,
          as I wandered room to room.

The packrats and the squirrels
          had been busy, I could see,
and they really hadn't left too much
          of interest to me.

'til I came upon an inner room,
          much darker than the rest,
where, on a nearly hidden ledge
          I found a wooden chest.

I picked it up with trembling hands
        and carried it outside,
though I knew just from the weight of it
        there wasn't much inside.

As I pulled off my bandana,
        and wiped the surface clean,
I saw it was a type of wood
that I had never seen.

And carved into the sides of it,
        were figures plain to see,
that seemed to have some meaning,
        though it wasn't clear to me.

I quickly pried the lid off,
        and took a peek inside,
but was filled with disappointment,
        which I didn't try to hide.

An old gourd wrapped in snakeskin,
        with a handle made of bone,
trimmed with rattles from some rattlesnakes
        and small carvings made of stone.

It was just a shaman's rattle,
         though a fancy one at that.
And I wondered if that snakeskin
         would make a hatband for my hat.

For, as I looked it over,
         it seemed to be near new.
and I assumed that snugly fitting lid
         had kept out dust and dew.

But as I grabbed the handle,
         my hand grew numb with cold,
and no one had to tell me
         that the thing was very old.

Still, I pulled it out and shook it,
         which was sure a big mistake.
For the noise it made grew louder,
         and the walls began to shake.

The rattling turned to thunder,
         then lightning split the sky,
and heavy rain began to fall
         on earth that had been dry.

I shoved that rattle in the chest,
      and jammed the lid on tight,
and felt a little better
      when the thing was out of sight.

I put it back upon that ledge,
      then quickly rode away,
through rain that kept on pouring down
      for hours more that day.

I haven't gone that way again.
      I always go around.
But through the years I've wondered,
      just what it was I found.

For I've heard people talking
      about more rain than the norm,
and how it seemed to come from nowhere,
      that unexpected storm.

III.

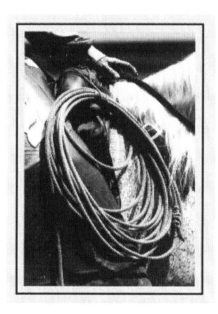

But I think we'll travel on a bit, beyond those
mountains there.
And maybe find a better place. There must be one
somewhere.

HORSES

I fell in love with horses,
      when I was pretty small,
and guess I'll always love them,
      no matter how things fall.

And I figure up in heaven
      every horse will have a stall.
Cause a heaven without horses,
      won't seem heavenly at all.

THE DESERT

The only desert that some men see,
       has buzzards perched on a lifeless tree,
where the burning sun makes a hell by day,
      and beads of sweat just dry away.

Where creosote trees line bone-dry streams,
      and mirages mock a cowboy's dreams.
Where gila monsters, lizards, snakes,
      are enough to give a strong man shakes.

Where there's little water, and less to eat,
      except saguaro, yucca, or mesquite.
And blistering sand with a blinding glare,
      leaves only death to be found there.

But I know a desert of a different kind,
      with mysteries and wonders to enchant
        the mind.
Like red sunsets over purple sage,
      or cliff dwellings built in a different age,

Animal tracks on a narrow trail,
     the thrumming flight of a flock of quail,
the silent glide of a hunting owl,
     and the lonesome sound of a coyote's howl.

Or the upright stance of the prairie dog,
     near a cottontail's home in a hollow log.
The full moon turning things at night,
     to a wonderland of pure delight.

Oh, the buzzards and snakes are there, all right,
     and death is waiting just out of sight,
for that careless move that might be made,
     when it's one hundred twenty degrees in the
          shade.

But a thousand things are worth the risk,
     like the desert smell when the air is brisk,
or the sudden blooms that come in hours,
     after one of those rare summer showers.

Yes, I know a desert that few men know.
     A place where only the strong can grow.
And I hope someday before I die,
     I'll live once more under a desert sky.

TRAVELING

My eyes were partly open when Pa told me to get up.

He had a fire going and hot coffee in his cup.

Ma was cooking breakfast. It was buffalo again.

That's all that we'd been eating since that old

        bull wandered in.

I went out in the bushes, where I did my morning thing,

then shivered as I washed up with cold water from the

        spring.

Next I brought the cow in from where the hobbles let her

        roam.

I don't know why I bothered; she'd been dry since

        we left home.

Pa and I hooked up the team before we stopped to eat,

and after we did dishes, helped Ma climb up to

        her seat.

By then false dawn was over, and the sky was

        getting bright.

I got my first good chance to see the place we'd spent

        the night.

The rain was really pouring when we'd stopped to
          make our camp,
and I really hadn't seen much with the light from
          our old lamp.
Now, as we started moving, I quickly looked around,
Where I saw a bunch of pinion trees and lots of
          muddy ground.

The spot looked pretty nice to me. The spring was
          clean and pure.
And any place that we could stop looked good to me
          for sure.
It seemed like we'd been on the move forever and a day.
It also seemed like I'd been walking almost all the way.

The wagon was too heavy, so I had to walk behind.
I guess I fibbed a little when I said I didn't mind.
But Ma in her condition couldn't walk too far at all,
Cause she just might lose the baby that was coming in
          the fall.

Pa had grown up farming, but said our land had all
          gone bad,
and told us we were moving far away from what we had.

He couldn't seem to find a place he thought would grow
                things right,
So we kept right on a traveling over every hill in sight.

By now I wasn't much surprised when some
                place wouldn't do,
and Pa said we were moving on in search of
                something new.
The weather either got too cold or else it got too hot.
I think he liked the looking more than finding us a spot.

Though Ma had liked a place or two, Pa hadn't picked
                a one.
And my advice was never asked about what we had done.
I'd have stayed most any place. We'd traveled far enough,
But getting Pa to listen up was really kind of tough.

And then we found a valley that was wide and fairly long.
The river down the middle had a current full and strong.
By gosh, the place was perfect, as far as I could tell,
and the happy look upon Ma's face said she was
                pleased as well.

Pa didn't say a single word, just slowly looked around,
then grabbed a shovel from the back and stuck it in the
       ground.
He knelt and sifted out some dirt, then smelled and
       tasted it.
But he didn't start in talking until he'd sat there for a bit.

At last he said, "This isn't bad. By far the best we've seen.
That river must run year around, and the water sure
       looks clean.
But I think we'll travel on a bit, beyond those
       mountains there.
And maybe find a better place. There must be one
       somewhere."

Ma didn't say a single word as she climbed down
       from her seat,
tugged our tent down from the wagon so it landed at
       Pa's feet.
Then she said, "You go on looking for a place that may
       not be.
As for me, I think I've found the spot my home is going
       to be."

A COWBOY'S LIFE

A cowboy's life sure ain't much fun,
        when storm clouds chase away the sun,
and the cows you're herding like to roam,
        while the horse you're on keeps heading home.

Riding the fence line ain't no joke,
        though a little bit better than being broke,
and a tarpaper shack is a welcome sight
        after riding all day and half the night.

When the foreman thinks your pay's too high
        for a chance to sleep out beneath the sky,
where the coyotes howl to hear a sound,
        and your softest bed is a piece of ground.

Where an evil, wild-eyed, long-horned steer
        will gore your horse just for coming near.
And you hope you're never set afoot
        by a prairie dog hole or a hidden root.

And cougar tracks, or the smell of a bear
       can give both you and your horse a scare,
So your nervous fingers start to beg
       for the rifle riding beneath your leg.

Yet once in a while you'll draw your pay
       and ride to a town not too far away,
Where you'll brag to cowboys just like you,
       how proud you are of what you do.

COMANCHE

They came down off the cap rock
    moving quiet,
        but something made her turn her head to look.
Then she grabbed her younger sister
    and ran toward the house,
        worried about how long that journey took.

As she hurried through the doorway,
    she turned her head to check,
        and guessed that they were two Comanche braves.
She was sure that they had seen her
    before she reached the house.
        And she'd heard of what they did to female slaves.

The heavy door slammed quickly;
    the bar dropped into place,
        though she knew that wouldn't stop them long at all.
So she grabbed her father's shotgun
    from the rack above the door,
        then peered out through the gun port in the wall.

They were headed toward the river,
  and she thought they might go by,
    'til the front one spoke and pulled his horse aside.
She saw the old one shake his head,
  say something in return,
    shrug, and then continue with his ride.

The young one's hair was black as night.
  and braided down his back.
    A loincloth was the only thing he wore.
She stared in fascination
  at his muscles when he moved,
    for she'd never seen an undressed man before.

He looked directly at her
  where she stood behind the port,
    but she couldn't move a muscle as she stared.
When he turned and rode toward her
  and the shotgun that she held,
    she knew that she could shoot him if she dared.

But her trembling hands were sweaty
  and she found she couldn't breathe
    as he stopped his horse not fifteen feet away.

Though she couldn't understand him
   as he slowly spoke some words,
     she somehow knew just what he meant to say.

His dark eyes held her blue ones
   for a moment lost in time
     and she felt her life would never be the same.
She was just a farmer's daughter,
   while he was a wild thing,
     something that no girl could ever tame.

He sat there for a while,
   then wheeled his horse around
     and rode toward the river and his friend.
She watched him as he rode,
   his head held high and proud,
     and prayed he'd never come her way again.

WHO GETS TO RIDE

When the chores are done, and the horses fed,
  but it's not yet time to go to bed,
I sit outside against the wall
  and listen to the night-birds' call,
and wonder how the fates decide,
  who has to walk, and who gets to ride.

TWILIGHT AT THE WATERHOLE

When the sun goes down in the desert
            and the light begins to fade,
then it's twilight at the water hole
            where animals parade.

The thieving ways of a young raccoon
            while a possum just plays dead.
The graceful swoops of a swallow
            as it feeds far over head.

The yap, yap, yap of a coyote comes
            from atop some distant hills.
And the painful yelp of a young wolf cub
            at the sting of a porcupine's quills.

There's a cautious step from a wily fox
            and the leap of a kangaroo rat.
Through the rising mist of a cloud of gnats
            comes the dart of a feeding bat.

There's the sudden pause of a mountain lion
　　　　at the call of a hidden quail.
Or the silent rush of a hunting owl
　　　　past a bobcat's stubby tail.

The hop, hop, hop of a rabbit,
　　　　or the hesitant step of a deer,
lured on by the water there
　　　　when thirst overcomes their fear.

'Til a campfire lights the shadows,
　　　　or a carelessly muttered word,
changes the whole scene quickly,
　　　　where nothing is seen nor heard.

CHAMPION

I rode the bad ones, and I rode the good,
    even rode some that no one else could.
I made lots of money by being the best,
    and lived my life hard without stopping to rest.

But years keep on passing. I'm no longer spry.
    My bones seem to ache when there's clouds in the sky.
The horses I draw are the worst in the state,
    and it's no longer fun when they open that gate.

Hungry young cowboys are making life tough.
    The horses I ride all seem to be rough.
But I entered again, pride-driven, of course,
    and I'm through to the finals and drawn a rank horse.

I hardly can move; I'm so beat up and sore.
    I've made up my mind I won't do this no more.
But the good Lord be willing, I'll make this last ride.
    Then I'll retire and hang onto my pride.

COWBOY CONTEMPLATIONS

In the valley far below me,
      sunlight flashes from a stream,
and from somewhere up above me,
      I can hear an eagle scream,

when I'm high up on the mountain,
      where the trees refuse to grow,
cause the granite spires are barren
      due to freezing wind and snow.

As I sit there on my saddle,
      while I marvel at the sights,
that keep my poor mind reeling,
      during sometimes sleepless nights,

I gaze out at my world
      with its ever changing view,
and cannot help but wonder
      why things work the way they do.

Like when flowers thirst for water,
     there are showers every spring,
or when songbirds felt like soaring,
     way back when, they grew the wing.

And though rattlesnakes are legless,
     something teaches them to crawl,
while the sticky feet the fly has,
     let it walk upon a wall.

When the rivers must keep flowing,
     all the snow from winter melts,
and with cavemen growing colder,
     someone taught them to use pelts.

High upon the highest mountains,
     or on sea beds far below,
something always seems to thrive there,
     any place that you might go.

Like the panda bear loves bamboo,
     that it nibbles on for hours.
While the leaves of eucalyptus
     the koala bear devours.

And where desert sands grow dryer,
      camels never seem to mind,
while the buzzards all grow fatter
      on whatever they can find.

Yet, the way it all fits smoothly,
      much like soft gloves fit my hands,
makes me stop and wonder
      about who drew all the plans.

WILD MARE

I sold a bull and dropped him off near Dallas,
      and with my empty trailer, started back.
But I had to stop for gas near Amarillo,
      and ended up well off the beaten track.

I missed the on-ramp leading to the freeway,
      and went around the block for one more try,
But I learned about an auction at the fairgrounds,
      when I heard the auctioneer as I went by.

I thought that since I had an empty trailer,
      I might pick me up a bargain calf or two.
I'd also driven hard for several hours,
      and felt the need for something else to do.

I found a place to park my truck and trailer,
      then took a seat where I could see the ring.
But the bargains that I hoped for all were taken,
      so I didn't make a bid on anything.

I heard a lot of noise outside the grandstands,
      and waited just to find out what was wrong.
A pretty mare came charging through the entrance,
      with several cowboys being dragged along.

Her shiny coat was nearer gold than buckskin.
      Her mane and tail were black as they could be.
As she stood there, breathing hard from her exertion,
      she was sure a lovely, lovely sight to see.

Now I've been riding horses near to always,
      and they're just a way to get the cow work done.
And only two or three I thought were special,
      but that mare that I was seeing sure was one.

I began to calculate my whole life's savings,
      in hopes that I might somehow make a bid.
But I knew that I was short by several hundred,
      unless that mare had faults that were well hid.

Then the auctioneer said, "Folks you sure are lucky.
      The owner of this mare has got to sell.
Though I'm starting out the bid at seven hundred,
      she's worth much more than that as you can tell.

I felt my spirits sag at such a number.

    I couldn't scrape that much up in a week.

So I bit my tongue and held my breath a little.

    My lack of money wouldn't let me speak.

The silence of the place was overwhelming,

    as I walked down front to get a better look.

But unless I found some valid reason not to,

    I wanted her no matter what it took.

The auctioneer said, "Folks it's highway robbery.

    But I'll drop her down two hundred if I must.

Since it's obvious she's worth at least two thousand.

    Someone will pay five hundred bucks I trust."

Once again it seemed that no one there was bidding,

    and it made me wonder what the heck was wrong.

It was clear these folks knew something that I didn't,

    but they weren't prone to passing it along.

So I jumped the fence to get a little closer,

    and heard somebody gasp up in the crowd.

That mare just stood there trembling with excitement,

    while she held her pretty head up high and proud.

Then a cowboy on a rope said, "Let me warn you.
    If you get too close in front, she tends to bite.
She'll also try to kick whoever's near her,
    and it doesn't seem to matter, left or right."

I asked, "What else is wrong that I should know of?
    What's keeping all these folks from bidding high?"
He said, "It's just they know that she's an outlaw.
    and came darned close to making someone die."

Now I'd run across some horses men called outlaws,
    and I knew a trick or two to tame them down.
I thought that I could tame this pretty filly,
    if I bought her and could get her out of town.

The auctioneer was saying, "I'll take two fifty,"
    when I whirled around and yelled, "You've got
    a deal."
As I paid the man with money from my pocket,
    I figured I had really made a steal.

Then a cowboy quickly roped her trembling front legs,
       and another from behind her roped the back,
while those on either side were being careful,
       to see she didn't get a bit of slack.

They put a blindfold on her in a jiffy,
       and after that she seemed to calm right down.
It was then I heard a sigh come from the bleachers,
       and it seemed to come from everyone around.

Those cowboys helped me put my halter on her,
       and took the time to lead her all about.
One said, "Make sure you put that blindfold on her,
       And calm her down before you let her out."

As I turned around and headed for my pickup,
       a cowboy stood there leaning on the door.
Upon his face he wore a strange expression,
       as he said, "I can't keep quiet anymore.

"I know I should have spoken up much sooner,
       before you had a chance to waste your dough.
But my conscience wouldn't let me rest this evening,
       if I didn't warn you now before you go.

"My neighbor Jim is known the whole state over,
          for raising horses classed as A-1 stock.
And everyone will tell you if you ask them,
          the man is just as steady as a rock.

"He bred and raised the mare that you just paid for,
          and thought she was the best he'd ever seen.
But he didn't know she'd turn out such an outlaw.
          To tell the truth that mare is just plain mean.

"Why once she bit and nearly tore his arm off.
          Another time she broke a rib or two.
Twice she's kicked the whole side off his horse barn,
          and that was when the thing was nearly new.

"He brought a team of experts in to train her,
          guys who thought they really knew their stuff.
But it wasn't long before they both admitted,
          that what they knew just wasn't quite enough.

"Everyone around has heard the stories.
          That's why they wouldn't bid a decent price."
"Well, thank you, sir," I told him, with a handshake.
          "I appreciate you being so darn nice."

"But since I've got her loaded I'll still take her.
          Maybe when she's older she'll calm down."
I said, "Goodbye," and climbed up in my pickup,
          then quickly made my way on out of town.

I drove all night to make it home by sun up,
          and put her in my very strongest stall.
Then after forking down some hay to fill her manger,
          took that blindfold off and hung it on the wall.

The trip had been a really long and hard one,
          so I went to bed and slept the day away.
'til my wife came in and woke me up for dinner,
          I'd forgotten that the day was Saturday.

My daughter Jill turned twelve years old last summer,
          and I'll confess that she's the apple of my eye.
When she didn't come to greet me same as usual,
          I turned toward my wife and asked her why.

She said, "Oh, you know her. She got up early.
          As she does when she don't have to catch the bus.
She went down to the barn right after breakfast.
          And when I make her come to eat she'll fuss."

I turned and quickly dashed out through the back door,
        Without waiting for my boots or hat or stuff.
All I had on was my stockings and my long johns,
        But I knew that that would have to be enough.

Well, I found her on the fence outside the horse stalls,
        and she had her brand new saddle by her side.
When I saw that she was still alive and healthy,
        I must admit I very nearly cried.

She jumped down to the ground and said, "Oh, Daddy.
        She's the kind of horse I've always dreamed about.
I can't wait to show her off to all my girlfriends.
        I know that Mary Lou will really pout."

Then I said, "I know she's very pretty, Honey.
        But I'm afraid she's much too wild for you to ride.
She might even be the kind that can't be gentled.
        A couple darned good men already tried.

"So I hope you understand me when I tell you,
        that you're not allowed to ride her right away."
She just laughed at me and said, "Oh, don't be silly.
        Don't you know that I've been riding her all day?"

IV.

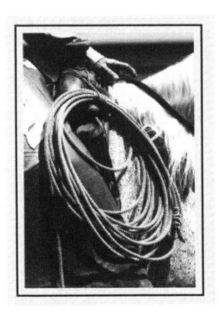

Who would have thought that an innocent kiss,

would lead to my world going crazy like this?

FRONTIER COURTSHIP

I wish that I could ride across the prairie,
 with no one there but just my horse and me,
until I reached the mountains in the distance,
 the mountains that from here I cannot see.

And when I got there, I would slowly climb them,
 until I stood upon the highest peak.
With arms outspread, I'd turn to look around me
 while praying for the happiness I seek.

I've wondered what the coming days would be like,
 and hoped I'd feel a lover's sweet caress.
Ma is calling to me now from the kitchen,
 "It's time that you put on your wedding dress."

I'm surrounded by the room that I grew up in,
 and know my life will change when day is done.
I hear the wagons coming down the driveway,
 where Pa is out there greeting everyone.

At last I finish dressing for my wedding,
    and the heavy veil sure makes things hard to see,
as I open up the doorway to my future,
    I hope I like the man they've picked for me.

COWGIRL

Now I've seen women working on a cow ranch
  and doing things that cowboys mostly do.
I've seen them riding hard and roping cattle,
  and some of them were darned good at it too.

I tried to judge them by the way they did the job,
  just like I would have any other hand.
But I must admit there was one little cowgirl
  who did some things I couldn't understand.

Cause though it might have seemed a little strange to me,
  to see a woman in the mud and dirt,
while wearing high-topped boots and them old blue-jeans,
  and Stetson hat and sweat-stained cowboy shirt,

It didn't bother me she rode the rough ones
  as good as me or any other hand.
And it didn't bother me that at the round up,
  she could castrate, notch them ears, or even brand.

No, it didn't bother me she'd do so many things,
  then conjure up a real good meal to boot.
What bothered me was how she did those manly chores,
  and at the same time always looked so cute.

GOLDEN OPPORTUNITY

They had a little place in south Missouri
    that barely kept the hogs and chickens fed.
He dreamed of leaving everything behind him
    and going west to look for gold instead.

But he had a pretty wife and seven children
    he'd have to say goodbye to if he went.
And he didn't have the cash to buy supplies with,
    cause every dime he made was quickly spent.

He said, "We need more land to make a living.
    Good bottomland like Hugo Summers got.
If I could find some money, I'd buy his place,
    and add it on to ours once it was bought."

His wife said, "Mr. Summers won't be selling.
    He's worked too hard to fix his land up right."
He said, "That man's been lonely since his wife died.
    I've seen his lamp a burning late at night."

"I think that maybe, if I had the money,
        he just might sell and move to somewhere new.
There ain't no single women close around here.
        So you never know what he is apt to do."

Then Sunday, after church, he heard men talking,
        about the gold found out near Sutter's Fort.
Gold was there to find on every mountain.
        At least that's what the rumors did report.

But when he told his wife, she said, "You're crazy.
        Most men never ever find no gold.
And even if you did, it'd take forever.
        The kids would all be grown, and I'd be old."

He said, "You know that James can feed the livestock
        He's been helping me since he was ten
The twins are big enough to do the harvest,
        though I expect to be back home by then."

She begged him not to go, but he ignored her,
        caught up in the passion of the day.
He bartered for enough to buy supplies with,
        and soon was ready to be on his way.

The night before he left, she fixed his dinner,
    with apple pie she'd baked that afternoon.
Then held him real close, and said she'd miss him,
    and hoped that he would come back very soon.

Next morning, as he sat upon his plow horse,
    he told her not to worry none at all.
That Hugo Summers said he'd gladly help her,
    and if she needed something, she should call.

After he was gone, she heated water,
    then took a bath and washed her pretty hair,
then said to James, "You go find Mr. Summers.
    Tell him we've got apple pie to spare."

AN INNOCENT KISS

Who would have thought that an innocent kiss,
 would lead to my world going crazy like this?
Where her brothers and cousins and uncles and dad,
 seem to think I have stolen the best thing they had.

Lucky for me, she slipped out that night,
 and warned me in time that I could take flight.
I kissed her goodbye and then rode away,
 cause both of us knew that I couldn't stay.

I learned they had friends all over the west,
 and some of their guns were known as the best.
So I changed my name and then headed east,
 hoping to live for a short time at least.

I learned how to shoot and practiced my draw,
 'til I wasn't afraid of the strangers I saw.
Then I got a job and earned a good name,
 but each hour that went by kept on seeming the same.

While I spent my days planning getting rich schemes,
>   the taste of her lips kept on haunting my dreams.
My heart kept on telling me what I didn't know,
>   'til at last I admitted that I had to go.

A year had gone by when I headed west,
>   hoping the sight of her might let me rest.
As I ride up the trail that leads to their spread,
>   I know there's a chance that I'll soon be dead.

I step from the saddle and knock on the door,
>   and find I'm more nervous than I've been before
Her father looks older than one year ago.
>   His face is more lined, his hair white as snow.

He says, "She was sure you would come back someday,
>   and I'll never have peace until she gets her way.
I've fought with my daughter for one solid year,
>   and I'll have to admit I 'm sure glad you are here."

MARSHAL

The stage was running hours late,
      and no one was around,
when the driver pulled it to a stop
      and jumped down to the ground.

As he helped her from the stagecoach,
      I caught a glimpse of shoe,
And I figured that without those heels,
      she'd stand about five-two.

The parasol she carried
      cast a shadow on her face,
and the dress that she was wearing
      looked a little out of place.

It was getting late that afternoon,
      the hottest part of day,
and I watched her as she stood there
      while the stage went on its way.

I was sitting on a wooden chair
      propped back against the wall
of the place that served as court, and jail,
      and local meeting hall.

As she slowly turned and walked toward
      the sidewalk where I sat,
I rocked my chair up forward,
      stood up and doffed my hat.

When she stopped to look me over,
      I said, "Can I help you, ma'am."
"She said, "Are you the marshal?"
      I answered, "Yes, I am."

The reason I was marshal,
      was I wore the fastest gun,
plus no one else would take the job,
      when all was said and done.

A lawman sure was needed
      when those cattle drives came through.
but as soon as they had moved on by,
      there wasn't much to do.

She stared at me a moment,
　　　　then reached into her bag,
brought out a two shot Derringer,
　　　　　partly wrapped up in a rag.

I made a lunge, and grabbed her,
　　　　but that didn't make her stop,
so we wrestled for a moment,
　　　　then fell down with me on top.

I grabbed that gun and twisted
　　　　'til she had to let it go.
It was then that I become aware
　　　　we were touching head to toe.

I'd been taught to be polite
　　　　to women half my size,
so my first impulse was let her up
　　　　and then apologize.

But she'd just tried to shoot me,
　　　　and might have another gun,
so I kept her pinned down to the ground,
　　　　'til my careful search was done.

Her face turned red, and so did mine,
   as she gasped in stunned surprise,
and I was so embarrassed,
   that I couldn't meet her eyes.

But at last I helped her to her feet,
   and locked her in a cell,
then made a pot of coffee,
   with fresh water from the well.

A couple cups had calmed me some,
   before I asked her why.
She put her face down in her hands,
   and then began to cry.

"Because you killed my father."
   Her sobbing voice was low.
"You shot him when he rode through here,
   fourteen months ago."

"What makes you think I killed him?"
   I asked her to explain.
She said, "They brought him home to me,
   days later on the train.

"and when I asked what happened,
        they said you shot him down.
That they hadn't caused no trouble,
        and were riding out of town."

I said, "I think they lied to you,
        if what I've heard is right,
though I wasn't here to see it.
        I was out of town that night."

"Back then I wasn't marshal,
        just a cowboy riding through.
But the fight that killed your father,
        killed old Marshal Stevens too."

"I know you won't believe me,
        but the record's plain and clear,
according to the Town Gazette,
        and I have a copy here.

I gave her time to read it,
        while I made my evening rounds,
surprised that I could only hear
        the normal small-town sounds.

I stopped to talk to people,
      that I met along each block,
and found that I was trapped between
      a hard place and a rock.

I learned no one had witnessed
      our encounter on the street,
and she seemed to be the type of girl
      your folks would like to meet.

I had a reputation
      as the fastest gun around,
and if I said she tried to shoot me,
      they would laugh me out of town.

So, after she apologized,
      I took her from that cell,
and rented her a place to stay
      in the Cattleman's Hotel.

Next day I saw her seated on
      the next stage headed west,
then sat down on my wooden chair
      to get a little rest.

I sat there and I watched the stage
       that carried her away,
and wondered what she'd say to me,
       if I called on her someday.

WATER STOP

I was standing by the loading pen,
      as she climbed from the train.
Her long black hair was braided,
      and the dress she wore was plain.

Her large hat cast a shadow,
      so I couldn't see her clear,
when she spoke to the conductor,
      who was piling luggage near.

He turned and pointed my way,
      as he sat the last piece down.
I wondered if she'd stay out there,
      or ride on into town.

Cause I figured she was headed
      to the Devlon's Two bar D,
and the ride she was expecting,
      wasn't there for her to see.

The place was just a water stop,
        some thirty miles from town.
And though we used it to load cattle,
        there wasn't much around.

A horse that I had purchased,
        was to be unloaded there.
A stallion I had bargained for
        down at the county fair.

The conductor was a friend of mine,
        who asked, "You want your horse?
Cause if you don't, I'll take him,
        for a reasonable price of course."

I laughed and said, "Not hardly, Joe.
        You couldn't afford his feed.
Besides, I think his bloodline is
        exactly what I need."

"Then let's not waste more time," he said.
        "We're running late today.
As soon as he's unloaded,
        we'll be on our way."

Once we had the ramp in place,
    I led that stallion out,
and when we had the ramp secured,
    I saw Joe look about.

He said, "I guess Tom sent you,
    to pick up his new bride.
But you should have brought a buggy,
    cause she's not dressed to ride."

"Is she the bride?" I asked him.
    "I haven't met her yet.
But this stallion is the only thing,
    I came down here to get.

"Something must have happened
    for Tom to be this late.
More likely it's a mix-up,
    and this isn't the right date.

"If he's just late she's apt to be
    a very angry bride.
But, I guess we'd better tell her,
    that she doesn't have a ride."

I tied my horse to a nearby post,
     then we walked to where she stood,
and I got my first close look at her,
     and she looked very good.

Joe said, "Miss Merriweather.
     This here is Jim McCay.
He's not here to pick you up,
     so I don't know what to say.

"You'll have to ride to town with me,
     or wait out here with Jim.
He used to be a ranger,
     so you'll be safe with him."

She nodded at me, while I stared at her
     and couldn't turn away.
I saw her frown, then shake her head,
     like she didn't know what to say.

To keep on staring would be rude,
     so I glanced down at the ground.
Then as the silence lengthened,
     I began to look around.

I said, "There's dust on the Two Bar road,"
       and pointed at the pass.
"I'll bet that's Tom and his buggy,
       because it's coming this way fast."

She stared at the dust, then glanced at Joe,
       then looked at me with a smile.
"If you think that's him, then I'll wait here.
       That can't be more than a mile."

"It'll take at least an hour," I said,
       "There are switchbacks on that ridge.
Then he'll have to go up stream a ways,
       to get across the bridge."

We stood and watched the train go on,
       then moved to the only shade,
in the shadow of the water tank,
       where benches had been made.

"So you were a Texas Ranger," she said,
       "How come you're not one now?"
"Well, Dad passed away, and Mom's too frail,
       to rope and brand a cow."

I thought I saw a twinkle
       in her pretty hazel eyes,
when she asked, "Are ranger stories true,
       or are they mostly lies?"

"That all depends," I told her,
       "on whom you listen to.
If told to impress a pretty girl,
       they might not be so true."

"Did you like the job?" she asked me,
       like she really wanted to know.
So we talked about my lawman days,
       for a quarter hour or so.

Then I asked her all about her life,
       and what she liked to do.
I felt as though I'd known her
       for at least a year or two.

That dust kept getting closer,
       while I wished it would disappear,
because I recognized Tom's buggy,
       when it finally got near.

Tom Devlon was a life-long friend,
      I usually liked to see,
but I didn't want him there at all,
      while she sat next to me.

I wanted to tell her how I felt,
      but knew I didn't dare,
when the man that she was promised to,
      was very nearly there.

We stood and watched as Tom drove up
      and jumped down from his seat.
I turned my back because I did not
      want to see them meet.

I heard him say, "I watched the train,
      and thought that's where you'd be.
I didn't know that Jim was here
      to keep you company."

"Hi, Jim," he said, so I turned around
      and quickly shook his hand.
He said, "I hoped that you'd get back,
      in time to be best man."

I looked at her, and she said to me,

"Then we can talk again soon.

I'm staying around while Beth and Tom

are on their honeymoon."

GREEN-EYED GIRL

I'd been an honest cowhand,
        working hard to earn my pay,
'til my boss's lonely widow
        sold the ranch away.

Times were tough, and jobs were scarce,
        and I was feeling down,
that cold and windy morning,
        when I saw that little town.

Since I was broke and hungry,
        I decided to go bad,
'cause I figured being hunted,
        was no worse than what I had.

I quickly walked into the bank,
        bandana tied in place,
cause I didn't want the banker
        to describe my homely face.

I'd watched him while he opened up,
   and kept track of those who came,
then counted those who left,
   until the number was the same.

The street was empty when I moved,
   not a soul in sight,
as I stepped inside that little bank
   and swung the door shut tight.

I'd pulled my gun when I stepped in
   and turned toward the cage.
But the man was gone, and in his place,
   was someone half his age.

And I could scarce believe her eyes,
   for they were brilliant green.
And without a doubt, the face I saw,
   was the prettiest one I'd seen.

She didn't flinch, or scream, or faint,
   or act the least bit shocked.
She said, "Pa went for coffee.
   I'm afraid the safe is locked."

For a moment, I just stood there,
     without a word to say,
then slowly backed toward the door,
     as I put my gun away.

"Wait," she said, "before you leave."
     Her voice was soft and low.
"I've got a proposition
     to make before you go.

"I've been stuck here all my life,
     and I don't want to stay.
I'll do anything you want,
     if you help me get away.

"There's a place to hide, right back there."
     She pointed to the rear.
"Where you can wait 'til Pa gets back.
     I'm sure he'll soon be here.

"You can take me hostage,
     and then give me half the dough.
I'll make it worth your while,
     and I don't care where we go."

Well, I turned around and bolted,
       as I pulled my kerchief down,
and quickly made it to my horse,
       then thundered out of town.

I rode hard for near two weeks,
       then found myself a job.
But I often think about that town
       and the bank I meant to rob.

I've faced outlaws, wolves, and snakes,
       and once a rabid squirrel.
But nothing scared me half as much,
       as that pretty, green-eyed girl.

FRONTIER WIFE

She was working in the garden
        late one sunny afternoon,
ready to stop hoeing,
        and start cooking dinner soon.

He crept out from the forest,
        like a ghost from some old grave,
and when something made her look up,
        she was facing a young brave.

He isn't wearing war paint,
        was the first thought that she had,
though she had no way of knowing
        whether that was good or bad.

She could feel her heartbeat pounding
        from the way he'd just appeared,
and it started beating faster
        as he very slowly neared.

There was no one at the ranch house
        to come charging to her aid,
but the hoe that she was holding
        had a newly sharpened blade.

So she gripped the handle tightly,
        as she tried to plan ahead.
She knew he'd probably grab it,
        if she swung it at his head.

All that he was wearing
        was a loin-cloth made of skin,
and she stared in fascination
        as he stepped forward once again.

She saw his muscles ripple,
        and could tell that he was strong,
then compared him to her husband,
        though she knew that that was wrong.

When he pointed to the horse-trough,
        and asked, "Water?" plain and clear,
she felt strangely disappointed
        after he stopped coming near.

He drank his fill, then thanked her,
  and soon disappeared from sight,
and her husband's meal was ready
  when he got home that night.

But, early the next morning,
  while the coffee water steamed,
she tried hard to forget about
  the things that she had dreamed.

ELIZABETH

He was tall, rich, and handsome,
        and a hero of note,
running for congress
        and assured of the vote.

While I was a cowman,
        with a very small spread,
just making a living
        with a few hundred head.

We both fell in love
        with Elizabeth Green,
the most beautiful woman
        who'd I'd ever seen.

But her family had money,
        and they knew I had none.
and they'd vote for him
        when the courting was done.

Yet, I knew she loved horses
      and I had a few.
Especially a young stallion,
      that was pleasing to view.

So I took her that stallion
      and showed him with pride.
Then spent fourteen days
      teaching her how to ride.

But her father won out,
      when he took her back east,
and I was alone,
      but knowing at least,

that she'd always remember
      our two weeks of love,
and those nights on a blanket
      with the stars up above.

BILL GRANGER

She was waiting for Pa by the wagon one day,
      while feeding the horses a handful of hay,
when a cowboy walked up, who just wanted to talk,
      and later convinced her to go for a walk.

Now, Jimmy MacCracken, at just seventeen
      was the best looking man that she'd ever seen,
and he soon held her hand as they walked about town,
      until Pa called her name while wearing a frown.

He told her MacCracken was part of a crowd,
      that was known to be wild, and reckless, and loud.
So she was not ever to see him again,
      cause Pa didn't want anything to begin,

She shouldn't have argued, cause she never had,
      and all that she did was make Pa very mad,
so that on the next trip, he left her behind,
      though the way things had been, she didn't
        much mind.

When Pa left out early, right after first light,
    she knew he'd be gone, until quite late that night,
so she finished her chores very early that day,
    then walked to the river, about two miles away.

She enjoyed the water, the birds, and the bees,
    'til she heard a horse coming, and hid in the trees.
She saw a young cowboy ride in from the west,
    in a battered old hat and brown cowhide vest.

She'd seen him before, at least once or twice,
    and as far as she knew, he was perfectly nice.
His name was Bill Granger, she'd heard someone say,
    and the ranch where he worked was a day's ride away.

They'd said he was shy, that he didn't mix much,
    but was great working horses and cattle and such.
Still, she kept herself hid, not sure what to think,
    as she watched him dismount and let his horse drink.

When he took off his boots, his hat, and his gun,
    she knew he'd be stripped before he was done.
And she had no desire to see a man bare,
    so she wanted to leave, but didn't quite dare.

She closed her eyes tight, for a minute or two,
      but couldn't help taking a peek at the view.
And she saw a broad back and shiny black hair,
      and a really quick glimpse of what else was there.

He dived in the river and started to swim,
      while she felt like saying hello to him.
But she didn't give in to the urges she had,
      'cause she didn't need Pa to know they were bad.

So she stayed where she was, until he rode away,
      then she realized it was now late in the day.
She hurried for home as the sun started down,
      quite happy that she hadn't gone into town.

Pa's dinner was ready when he got back that night,
      and she said she was sorry, and knew he was right.
He said, "I've been thinking about what I've done,
      by letting you grow up without enough fun.

"I think that it's time you made some new friends,
so we're having a party when branding-time ends."
She gasped in surprise, and felt somewhat numb,
as she heard herself say, "Can Bill Granger come?"

V.

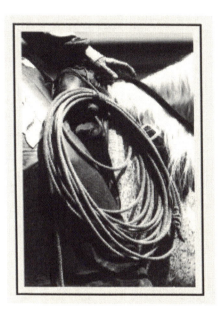

Charlie used to ride them bulls,
but me, I had more sense.
While he was out there riding,
I was sitting on the fence.

BILLY BOB

My friend, Billy Bob McCoy,
      was locked up by the sheriff,
when all he'd done was borrow someone's horse.

He'd had a few too many
      in a bar ten miles from home,
and was much too drunk to walk that far, of course.

I'd been to see my mama,
      who was feeling sort of poor,
so I didn't know a thing about his plight.

They had quickly found him guilty
      and sentenced him to hang,
which I learned when I reached town that
      Sunday night.

The boys were all at Harry's bar
      and were having quite a time
"We're hanging him at dawn," I heard one shout.

When I saw that brand new gallows
       they had built beside the jail,
I knew I had to figure something out.

I sneaked into the powder-house
       at Hopper's Peacock mine,
where I found some dynamite, a cap, and fuse.

But I was just a cowboy,
       and that's all I'd ever been,
so I didn't know how much I'd have to use.

That jail was made of river rock
       and good stout iron bars,
and there wasn't time for me to ask around.

But I figured it would maybe take
       at least a case or more,
to make those walls come tumbling to the ground.

The north side was too open
       and a widow lived behind
so I slipped in by the saddle shop next door.

Since a night guard was on duty,

    I quietly dug a hole,

then placed my charge beneath that jailhouse floor.

At last I got the fuse lit,

    then walked back to the street,

where I'd tied my horse when I got into town

Then I swung up in the saddle

    and rode about a block,

then stopped and slowly reined my horse around.

I must have left that fuse too long,

    for I'd almost given up,

before that dynamite at last cut loose.

And it seems I used a bit too much,

    for it blew the place to bits,

but at least old Billy Bob escaped the noose.

ROPER

Pa told me not to practice roping cattle,
       cause Ma would be upset if I got hurt.
So I nailed a couple cow horns to a sawhorse,
       and wrestled with that critter in the dirt.

But it wasn't very long 'til I was ready
       to handle something livelier than that.
So I spent awhile just roping our old cow dog,
       since I couldn't ever catch up with the cat.

But I couldn't get that dog to run for nothing.
       He just stood there with his head down
          near the ground.
And it wasn't any fun to try to chase him,
       when all he did was follow me around.

Then one day when Pa had gone to auction,
       and Ma was busy baking apple pie,
I thought that it was time for real roping,
       and to give that white-faced bull of Pa's a try.

Pa always kept him penned up in the cow-barn,
  and I knew I couldn't rope him there inside.
So first I turned him out into the pasture,
  where I'd have some room to swing my rope and ride.

I'd heard Pa saying something about a heifer,
  that he'd locked up in a nearby holding pen.
He thought that she was still too young for breeding,
  so was holding her 'til she came due again.

Though I could hear her bawling in the distance,
  I didn't really know what Pa had meant.
But that bull was awful anxious to be moving,
  and straight toward that holding pen he went.

I rode my Shetland pony up beside him,
  and my first cast with my rope went straight and true.
Then I quickly tied the loose end to the saddle,
  though I wasn't sure what else I had to do.

I must admit my pony tried his darnedest,
  when I pulled back on the reins with all I had.
That bull just wheeled around and started snorting,
  'cause all that we had done was make him mad.

He lowered down his head and started charging,
  and I knew my pony couldn't take a hit.
Those horns were not as long as some old longhorns,
  but long enough to hurt him quite a bit.

My pony must have sensed that things were desperate.
  He'd never run that fast since he was born.
But he couldn't go no faster than that bull could,
  'cause the rope was still tied tightly to the horn.

We made a couple circles around the henhouse,
  then cut a swath through Ma's new garden plot.
The bull had gained enough to give me leeway,
  and I managed to untie that pesky knot.

But being free just made that old bull madder.
  His beady eyes were glowing red with hate.
So we made another trip around the henhouse,
  then headed down the driveway toward the gate.

That heifer in the holding pen was bawling,
  and luckily the driveway went that way,
'cause the bull soon stopped to listen to her calling,
  and something seemed to make him want to stay.

I rode back to the house where Ma was waiting.
> She sent me to the shed to get the rake.
By the time I got the garden looking normal,
> I knew that I had made a big mistake.

While I worked, Ma walked down through the pasture,
> and grabbed my rope which that old bull still wore.
I guess he was tired from all that running,
> 'cause he didn't seem as frisky as before.

Ma made me take a bath, then fed me supper,
> and sent me up to bed when it got late.
But I saw some headlights turn in at the driveway,
> and waited while Pa opened up the gate.

I figured he'd come see me when she told him
> how I'd disobeyed him once again.
Later on I heard him in the kitchen,
> and Ma was saying something now and then.

I sneaked out to the stairs where I could hear them,
> while thinking maybe I should run away.
But I heard him telling Ma about the auction,
> and when he finished, ask, "How was your day?"

She said, "I baked a pie for Sunday dinner.

    while your son was roping everything in sight.

I think it's time you gave him real lessons,

    and taught him how to do the whole thing right.

"I figure he'll be safer roping heifers.

    'cause heaven knows what he might try instead.

And by the way, that heifer you've been holding.

    Well, turn her loose, cause she's already bred."

TAKE TIME

Take time to smell the roses,
            was what Henry Wadsworth said.
Or was it said by someone else,
            who's also long since dead?

That really doesn't matter,
            cause it sounds like good advice.
But the first time that I heard it,
            I was eating beans and rice

And sipping on tequila
            that was watered down with gin.
Take my word that I won't ever
            try that mix again.

Cause hearing such profound advice
            while three sheets to the wind,
is apt to make you do some things
            you never can defend.

I staggered through the bat-wings,
        but the sidewalk was too low.
With flailing arms and flying feet,
        I put on quite a show.

The horses at the hitch-rail,
        all made room for me to land,
as I skidded on my belly
        through the horse manure and sand.

Such aromatic mishaps weren't
        enough to change my mind.
I was headed for the Widow Jones's
        to see what I could find.

She lived in solo splendor
        in a little two-room shack,
and I'd heard she had some roses
        in her garden plot out back

I found her place my second try,
        or perhaps it was the third,
and tried to tiptoe through the gate
        to keep from being heard.

The hinges squeaked, the cowbell rang,
    the dog began to bark.
The Widow Jones yelled loudly,
    "Who's that out there in the dark?"

I quickly turned around to run,
    but tangled up my feet.
The next thing I remember,
    I was sitting on my seat.

The gate swung closed and somehow jammed,
    and I was trapped inside.
The dog was getting closer,
    and again the Widow cried,

"Who's that out there sneaking round?
    I'm warning you to scoot.
This shotgun's filled with buckshot,
    and I'm not afraid to shoot."

The gate was stuck. The dog was near.
    I heard those hammers click.
I figured I had better get
    behind that house real quick.

I took off like a greyhound
      that was more than slightly swacked.
It must have taken thirty steps
      to get my feet untracked.

But I made it to the corner,
      though I wasn't running straight,
and kept right on a going
      'til I reached another gate.

That dog was growling something fierce
      and sounding close behind.
And the latch to open up that gate
      was much too hard to find.

So I launched myself with graceful ease
      toward the topmost rung,
and for a short split second,
      that was where I hung.

Then like a diver's graceful swan,
      I floated for a while,
before smashing through some bushes
      and landing in a pile.

Limbs were snapping, bushes crashing,
and I heard my trousers rip.
I felt those rose-thorns grabbing hold
from toe to fingertip.

As I lay there in the darkness,
midst the bushes and the thorns,
feeling somewhat like a matador
impaled upon some horns,

I wondered how much peacefulness
a body could endure,
if he stopped to smell the roses,
and could just smell horse manure.

THE BATH

It couldn't quite be called a drought,
      but we hadn't seen much rain.
The sun was shining down so hot,
      it must have fried my brain.

I hadn't had a bath in days
      and needed quite a scrub,
when I saw that lonely windmill
      pumping water in a tub.

The land nearby was very flat,
      I could see for miles around.
So I knew no one would interrupt
      when I stepped down to the ground.

What once had been an old bathtub,
      was now a watering trough.
And that water looked so tempting,
      that I peeled my clothes right off.

I decided then I'd do things right
        and wash them all as well.
Though I knew the wait for them to dry
        might be quite a spell.

The ground had all been chopped up bad,
        by stock that came to drink
And not 'til everything was soaked
        did I take time to think.

There didn't seem to be a place
        to lay them out to dry.
The cleanest place that I could find
        was my pony standing by.

So I spread out on my saddle,
        everything that I had worn,
held there by my gun belt,
        which I looped around the horn.

My boots went in my saddlebags
        when I climbed into the tub,
where I lay and soaked awhile,
        and then began to scrub.

But I heard a noise behind me
      so I turned my head to look,
and saw a coyote chase a cottontail,
      and that was all it took.

Perhaps it was by some design,
      that they came straight my way,
but the ruckus they created,
      spooked my horse away.

I jumped right out, all dripping wet,
      and started in pursuit,
but that horse of mine had never seen me
      in my birthday suit.

He didn't seem to recognize me
      dressed in just my skin,
for every time that I got close
      he shied away again.

After somewhere near an hour,
      my skin was turning red,
my feet were leaving bloody tracks,
      and I wished that horse were dead.

It was then I made my mind up,
     just to shoot that zebra dun.
And the only thing that saved him
     was the fact he had my gun.

I knew I'd soon be blistered bad,
     if something wasn't done.
I had to find some sort of shade
     to hide me from the sun.

I saw a rock some three feet tall
     that cast a bit of shade,
So I stumbled to that narrow strip
     and that was where I stayed.

But I must have fallen fast asleep,
     for it was late that day,
when I woke up to find my horse
     was a mere ten feet away.

I must admit I was surprised
     he didn't turn to run,
when I slowly got up to my feet
     and approached that zebra dun.

Then I noticed that the reins were tied
        to some long-dead creosote.
And a cactus-thorn pinned to my pants
        held a roughly scribbled note.

It said, "I found your horse alone,
        and tracked him back to here.
I figured you would be all right
        if I left him standing near.

I didn't wake you up because
        you seemed to be done in.
But I think you'll feel much better
        when you get all dressed again."

Well, I brushed off all the dirt I could
        and put my clothes back on,
as I wondered what I had to do
        before I could be gone.

I planned to leave for China
        on the next slow-moving boat.
Cause the boss's pretty daughter
        was the one who wrote the note.

AFTERMATH

The aftermath of a frightened skunk,
      explained our dog being gone.
The aroma of that white striped beast
      in the bunkhouse lingered on.

We'd gone to town on Saturday night
      and ended up in jail.
But the cost of the food that we all ate,
      was enough to go our bail.

Some of the boys were a bit upset,
      that the marshal ruined our fun,
and grumbled some on the way back home,
      that something should be done.

But our brand new guest with the awful smell,
      quickly put those thoughts to rest,
as we tried to think about what to do,
      and decide whose plan was best.

It seems he'd found a place to stay,
        underneath the bunkhouse floor,
and every time that dog got close,
        he'd sprayed the place once more.

We had to take our beds outside,
        and move them well upwind.
The gagging stench he'd left behind,
        we thought would never end.

So we all drew straws just to see who lost,
        and the loser's task was clear.
Just crawl underneath with a long forked stick
        and not be stopped by fear.

Well it took awhile, but it all worked out,
        and the skunk was boxed up tight.
Then someone thought of the marshal again,
        and suggested we set things right.

The marshal lived on a one-room shack
        on a lot behind the jail,
and we all agreed that our plan would work
        so we soon were on the trail.

Perhaps the wind double-crossed us some,
       when our scent drifted on ahead,
but the marshal's gun left us little choice,
       so we raised our hands instead.

The box we had, with the skunk inside,
       was proof of our intent,
so he locked us up in an unused shack
       where it seems he paid the rent.

And what we'd done must have made him mad,
       cause he left us little pride,
when he opened up the door for a second,
       and tossed that skunk inside.

I GOTTA GO

Charlie used to ride them bulls,
        but me, I had more sense.
While he was out there riding,
        I was sitting on the fence.

The only reason I was there,
        was Charlie didn't drive.
So I'd take him in my pickup
        just to make sure he'd arrive.

Sometimes he won, sometimes the bull,
        sometimes he nearly died.
But he always seemed to bounce right back
        in time for his next ride.

The years went by and we got old
        and he don't ride no more,
But we still go to see the show
        and watch the good ones score.

We went to Old Town Clovis once
       when all the rides were done
And called on every bar we found
       'til sometime after one,

Then bought a couple cases just
       to help us keep on track.
And so as not to litter,
       threw the empty cans in back.

We hadn't gotten very far
       when Charlie said, "Oh. Oh.
You'd better find a place to stop,
       'cause man, I gotta go."

By then, most every place was closed,
       at least those with a head.
Charlie said, "I can't wait.
       I'll use a can instead."

He didn't give me time to stop,
       just opened up the door,
climbed around in back and
       grabbed an empty from the floor.

I was sure that he would fall,
        so quickly hit the brakes.
Sometimes a little thing like that
        is all disaster takes.

He cart-wheeled up above the cab,
        then bounced once off the hood,
and landed just beside the road
        like an old bull rider would.

I got her stopped, and staggered back,
        quite sure that he was dead.
"Man, that old bull was pretty mean,"
        were the only words he said.

I dragged him to the pickup,
        pushed him in amongst the cans,
then sat there for a moment
        as I quickly made some plans.

I knew that if the cops found out
        I'd do time on the rock,
so decided on a vet we knew,
        who doubled as a doc.

The vet had barely got in bed,
    and hadn't slept a wink.
I knew because in several bars
    I'd bought the man a drink.

He helped me get old Charlie out
    and carry him inside,
and said, "I told him years ago,
    he's too damn old to ride."

I didn't try to set him straight,
    cause what he didn't know,
he couldn't pass on to the law
    and I'd be free to go.

I sat around the waiting room,
    it seemed like half the night.
Until that vet came out and said,
    "I think he'll be all right.

'Except for those two broken legs
    he seems to be quite sound.
But he's going to need a wheelchair
    to help him get around."

"I've got a brand new 'lectric one
   I've had almost a year.
A patient didn't want it
   'cause it's only got one gear.

"Drive your pickup round in back,
   there by the loading dock.
You know the one I sometimes use
   to unload injured stock."

He showed me how to work the chair,
   'cause Charlie was still out.
I must admit I had some fun
   just driving it about.

But at last I got it lined up right
   and drove it up the ramp.
And then we carried Charlie out,
   though the plaster was still damp.

And as I looked him over,
   I knew I had a chore.
Those plaster casts were fitted
   from mid-thigh to the floor.

Before we had him settled in
    I somehow sprained my back.
But at last we got him propped
    between my toolbox and the jack.

The vet said, "Here's some pain pills.
    I've tried them out myself.
I'll throw them in for nothing.
    They've been too long on my shelf."

Charlie's eyes were open
    though they seemed a little glazed.
The fact that he was still alive
    was what had me amazed.

I opened him a cool one,
    just to help him make the ride,
then had a couple more myself
    before I climbed inside

And headed for the foothills,
    where old Charlie had his spread.
I had the choice to take him there,
    or home with me instead.

The curves were getting tighter,
        and I was driving slow,
when Charlie pounded on the cab
        and yelled, "I gotta go."

I saw an unused loading pen,
        with an outhouse near the gate.
I figured that was more humane
        than making Charlie wait.

Besides, there was a loading ramp,
        which gave me food for thought.
We could use that fancy wheelchair
        that Charlie's money bought.

I somehow got him in the seat,
        though it really pained my back.
As he headed down that ramp, I said,
        "Keep the thing on track."

Now it didn't cross my mind that
        Charlie hadn't been awake,
when that vet had showed me how to start,
        and turn and steer and brake.

By the time he reached the bottom,

  he was moving pretty good,

and headed straight toward the place,

  where that old outhouse stood.

I jumped down from the pickup

  but the landing jarred my back.

I folded to the ground just like

  an empty burlap sack.

But Charlie kept on going

  right on through that outhouse door.

As the walls began to crumble,

  well, I couldn't watch no more.

I kept my eyes shut tightly

  as I listened to the crash,

then only seconds later,

  heard a muffled splash.

I quickly struggled to my feet

  and hurried to the spot.

"Charlie. Charlie," I kept yelling,

  not sure he'd hear or not.

"I'm okay," he answered,
        "There ain't no need to shout.
Get a lasso from the pickup
        so you can pull me out."

I knew I couldn't lift him,
        so I backed the truck up near,
tied a lasso to the bumper
        and yelled so he could hear.

"Slip that noose around you,
        then let out with a shout.
It won't take but a minute
        to haul you safely out."

Well, it took a couple minutes,
        then I heard him loud and clear,
so I jumped back in the pickup
        and slammed the thing in gear.

As it took off with a sudden lurch,
        I felt a touch of doubt,
and looked back through the window,
        to see him topping out.

He'd tied that rope tight to the chair
    while sitting in the seat.
By the time I got that pickup stopped,
    I'd dragged him forty feet.

"Why'd you tie it to the chair?"
    I asked him with a frown.
"Well, hell," he said, "I couldn't stand
    to let the poor thing drown."

With water from a horse trough,
    and a bucket from the truck,
it took me several minutes
    to wash off most the muck.

By then I was getting sober,
    and my back was hurting bad,
but that jar of Charlie's pain pills
    was the only thing I had.

I briefly read the label.
    It said something about a steer.
But I took a couple anyway
    and washed them down with beer.

I pushed that wheelchair up the ramp,
>   with Charlie still astride.
I knew I couldn't lift him
>   to a better place to ride.

So I used that handy lasso
>   to attach him to the chair.
By the time I got the knots all tied,
>   he couldn't go nowhere.

I was feeling pretty happy
>   as I pulled out real slow.
Then Charlie banged upon the cab
>   And yelled, "I gotta go."

SAVING BUSTER

Buster was there,

with his stallion and mare,

> while I rode a gelding he'd loaned.

And I must admit,

I was jealous a bit,

> of the beautiful horses he owned.

We were working the brakes,

doing all that it takes,

> to get them old cows to come out,

with Buster's cow dog,

dodging log after log,

> taking orders by whistle or shout.

When out of the brush,

with a lightning fast rush,

> came an old longhorn bull on the prowl.

That dog took one look,

and that's all it took,

> as he turned and ran off with a howl.

Then Buster's horse started
to buc, and they parted,
    with Buster left sprawled on the ground.
With no place to hide,
and no horse to ride,
    I could see him look blankly around.

I was some yards away,
not involved in the fray,
    when that old longhorn bull made his play.
I grabbed at my gun,
spurred my horse to a run,
    though I knew I was too far away.

That bull was plumb crazed,
and Buster was dazed.
    I could tell by the way he just stood.
Since I couldn't stand by,
and see Buster die,
    I had to do all that I could.

Now, my skill with a gun,

from a horse at the run,

  is nothing I'd dare brag about.

But I still had to try,

or just watch my friend die,

  so I fired and gave out with a shout.

Then I opened my eyes,

and stared in surprise,

  as Buster's hat flew through the air.

He stood, looking at me,

somewhat shocked I could see.

  I could tell he was still unaware,

that that bull, which was large,

was now in full charge,

  so I raised up my gun once again.

From Buster's shocked look,

it was clear he mistook,

  the danger he thought he was in.

As I fired off a round,

he sprawled flat on the ground,

     and that bull just went thundering by.

And kept right on going

without even slowing,

     though believe me, I'll never know why.

Buster's hands shook,

as he gave me a look,

     and asked, "Tell me, how'd you find out?

"Cause you bet your life,

I never called on your wife,

     until sure you were nowhere about."

Well, I sat there a bit,

while the shock and pain hit,

     and thought about shooting him dead.

But I gave him his life,

and then gave him my wife,

     while I took his stallion instead.

FANNING FOOL

The reason I'd been losing
      wasn't hard to understand,
when I saw the local card-shark
      palm an ace to fill his hand.

The fact I was a stranger
      on my way just passing through,
didn't mean that I'd ignore
      what I had seen him do.

So I told him he was cheating,
      loud enough for all to hear,
and the place grew deadly quiet,
      as men backed away in fear.

I saw his right hand moving
      toward the gun I knew he had,
and figured what he planned to do
      could only turn out bad.

To have him threaten me like that,
          just wasn't very nice,
so I quickly grabbed my right-hand gun
          and fanned the hammer twice.

My first shot broke the whiskey bottle
          in the barkeep's hand.
The second hit a spittoon,
          that was partly filled with sand.

The man that I was shooting at,
          dove quickly to the floor.
So just to keep him moving,
          I fanned a couple more.

My third shot hit a lantern
          hanging up above the bar,
and I'm pretty sure the fourth one
          broke a half-filled pickle jar.

A cloud of smoke came blasting out
          to punctuate each shot.
By the time I fired the fourth time,
          I couldn't see a lot.

But since I couldn't tell for sure
        exactly how things stood,
I fired off my next two rounds
        just to prove I could.

As I tried to find my target
        through the powder smoke and gloom,
I heard a couple more shots,
        from somewhere in the room.

So I quickly grabbed my left-hand gun
        and started fanning it as well,
as I tried to keep from coughing
        from that acrid gun-smoke smell.

At last the place grew quiet,
        though I thought I heard a moan.
But as the smoke began to clear,
        I found myself alone.

I quickly punched out empties,
        putting new rounds in each gun,
cause I didn't know if I would have
        to fight some more or run.

The mirror back behind the bar
        was splintered all to bits.
It was quite apparent
        it had taken several hits.

The money on the table
        was what I might have won.
So I figured it was really mine,
        when all was said and done.

As I put it in my pocket,
        I slowly looked around,
and decided maybe it was time
        to find another town.

As I rode into the darkness,
        I was a wiser man,
and thought about those countless hours
        I'd practiced how to fan.

But I'd learned a real good lesson,
        before it was too late.
Fanning may be faster,
        but it sure ain't much for straight.

BILLY JOE AND ME

Some folks think that Billy Joe
    and me should be in jail.
While others would just like to see
    us run out on a rail.

But we're not really all that bad,
    just looking for some fun.
That fire was accidental,
    and it didn't hurt no one.

I must admit the preacher's horse
    did end up sort of lame,
but tossing firecrackers out
    was nothing but a game.

Those cinches that we almost cut
    belonged to passers through.
We figured that would bring a laugh
    to everyone in view.

And who'd of thought that only one-half
   stick of dynamite,
would blow the marshal's outhouse
   so completely out of sight?

The reason folks don't like us
   is all due to Mrs. Flynn.
She saw us sneaking through the brush
   and quickly turned us in.

The marshal grabbed us by the neck,
   and was marching us through town,
when shots rang out inside the bank
   and he said, "You boys get down."

Four robbers came a rushing out
   and mounted up real quick.
But all their cinches broke in two
   and dumped them off real slick.

The marshal had them rounded up
   and locked tight in a cell,
before old Mrs. Flynn came out
   and started in to yell.

"Them two rascals did it all."
    She pointed straight at us.
"I seen them cutting cinches
    and raising all that fuss."

The way the marshal looked at me,
    sure left me feeling sad.
To stand there without running,
    took all the nerve I had.

But then he said, "I heard the blast.
    It brought me back to town.
If it wasn't for these rascals,
    I wouldn't have been around.

"And cutting through those cinches,
    didn't turn out all that bad.
Folks with money in the bank
    are feeling pretty glad.

"As far as my old outhouse goes,
    it'd seen much better days.
I'd have had to tear it down
    and move it anyways."

As I listened to him talking,
    my mood improved a bit,
'til he said, "They'll feel much better,
    when they've dug me a brand new pit."

HANSONS' BAWDYHOUSE

The girls at Hansons' Bawdyhouse
      were finished for the night,
and everyone had gone to bed,
      and doors were locked up tight.

But a cowboy in a hurry,
      driven careless by desire,
had dropped a lighted cigar-butt
      that smoldered into fire.

An early morning riser
      smelled the smoke and gave alarm,
and the fire was soon extinguished,
      doing very little harm.

For the local volunteer brigade
      had practiced what to do,
and the damage was restricted to
      a fancy drape or two.

The Hanson girls were thankful
        that their house had not burned down,
so they offered cut-rate prices
        to every volunteer in town.

But most of them were married,
        and it upset all their wives.
Any husbands caught at Hansons' place
        were flirting with their lives

It was only four nights later,
        when they heard that awful cry.
The bawdyhouse was burning,
        and the glow lit up the sky.

This time they didn't save it,
        and it burned down to the ground,
cause one fireman, who was single,
        was the only one around.

Though someone muttered, "Arson,"
        any evidence was gone,
so the girls from Hansons' bawdyhouse
        thought it best that they move on.

The word was quickly passed on to
      each cattle ranch around,
and everyone was watching
      when the Hanson girls left town.

And though the legends tell us
      macho cowboys never cry,
more than one poor lonely cowhand
      wiped a teardrop from his eye.

About the Author:

Robert R. "Bob" Brown carried a gun for 33 years as a law enforcement officer before he retired from the California Highway Patrol. He began to write fiction in 1965 but switched to poetry and is now a popular cowboy poet. He has written over 500 poems, many of them short stories about the west.

His vision of the old west was influenced by Zane Grey, Max Brand, and Louis L'Amour, and that is the west he writes about.

Three of his poems appeared in the anthology COWBOY POETRY MATTERS by Story Line Press, edited by Robert McDowell. He enjoys reading dressed as a cowboy and has read his poetry on KVPR--Valley Public Radio and KVPT Television, as well as at poetry readings in Central California.

Bob and his wife Margaret have travelled from Alaska to Florida in their motor home, and have visited the states in which his characters have their adventures. During the Korean War, they lived in Tucson, Arizona where he learned to love the desert.

More Books Published by

Brave New Genre, Inc.

Novels by Bull Marquette:
The Fifth Plane
The Weatherman

Short Story Collections
(also by Bull Marquette):

Got 8 If You Want 'Em

These books, and others by a growing list of
authors available in Print-On-Demand or in E-
books at:

   bravenewgenre.com

and watch for more Cowboy Poetry by:
   Robert R. Brown.

Made in the USA
Lexington, KY
26 April 2011